AJ's
Best Friends

AJ's Best Friends

Karla Erickson

Illustrations
by Sandy F. Gagon

Bookcraft
Salt Lake City, Utah

All characters in this book are fictitious,
and any resemblance to actual persons,
living or dead, is purely coincidental.

Library of Congress Catalog Card Number: 93-73840
ISBN 0-88494-906-0

First Printing, 1993

Printed in the United States of America

Contents

1

Grandma's Secret

"Won't you tell me where we're going?" AJ asked her father as she climbed into the family Suburban. "And why aren't Jake and Josh coming with us?"

AJ's father just chuckled. "You'll find out," he said. "Your brothers have gone ahead, and they'll meet us."

AJ's mother was busy packing salads and sandwiches. *We're probably visiting some relatives,* AJ thought. *But why are Dad and Mom so secretive about it?*

"AJ," Jen called from the front porch, "did you lock the back door?"

"Yes," AJ answered. She watched her older sister, Jen, turn the lock on the front door and slam it shut. AJ had always thought Jen was the prettiest girl in high school. Her blonde hair glistened in the early morning sun.

I wish I were more like Jen, she thought. *No wonder she's a cheerleader. I wish I had her cute build. She's so short. She's so—*

Her thoughts were interrupted abruptly.

"Can I sit by the window?" Sara asked as she scooted inside the car. "It's my turn."

AJ moved over. "Sara, you could've taken the other side and sat by that window," AJ said. "Why do you always have to have everything I want?"

Sara flashed AJ a happy smile. Her dimpled cheeks enhanced her bubbly personality. "Thanks, AJ. You can sit by this window on the way home."

"Sara, do you know where Jake and Josh are?" AJ asked, changing the subject to avoid an argument.

"Nope," said Sara. "Dad just told me that we're going somewhere fun, and they'll be there, too."

"Hope you have a good book to read," AJ's mother said, as she climbed into the front seat. "This is going to be a long ride."

"Are we going to St. George?" AJ asked. Her mother always had them bring books to read when they went to St. George.

"You'll see," answered mother.

AJ pulled out her bag. Instead of reading, she decided to write her big brother, Benj, a letter. How she missed him! But she loved receiving his letters from Germany. He always told her about the investigators he was teaching and how great it was to be a missionary.

"Are you going to read?" Sara asked.

"Not right now," AJ answered. "I'm writing Benj a letter."

"Can I have some of your paper?" said Sara, her

big brown eyes wide with enthusiasm. "I can draw a picture for Benj."

AJ handed her some paper. Why did Sara have to do everything she did? *Sometimes little sisters can be a real pain,* thought AJ.

As they turned south on the freeway, AJ smiled. *I was right,* she thought. *We're going to St. George. It'll be fun to see Grandma and Miranda.*

AJ loved Miranda, her grandmother's golden retriever. She had always wished that someday she'd have a dog just like her.

As AJ tucked the finished letter to Benj inside her bag, she glanced at Sara.

"Dad!" AJ called. "I think we'd better stop. Sara looks like she's carsick."

Sara's face was pale, and she was holding her stomach. "I feel really sick," she moaned.

As soon as her father stopped the car on the side of the road, AJ reached across Sara and flung open the car door. "Hurry, get out in the fresh air," she said. "It'll help you feel better."

Her mother rushed over to Sara's side. AJ got back inside the car with Jen. "I don't know why she has to get carsick," said AJ. "It makes me feel sick."

"Me, too," agreed Jen. They broke out laughing as they saw each grimace at the thought.

"Don't be too hard on Sara," scolded their father. "I remember when you girls had the same problem. Sara will outgrow it, too."

"I just hope they brought something to spray inside the car so we don't have to smell her," Jen giggled to AJ.

AJ's mother overheard Jen's comment and glared

at her as she wiped Sara's face. Her glance told both Jen and AJ not to say another word.

When Sara crawled back into the car, she suddenly burst into tears.

AJ put her arms around her. "Don't worry, Sara," she said. "I know you don't like getting carsick. C'mon, let's both draw a picture to send Benj."

AJ pulled out the crayons and paper. It was pretty hard to be mad at her little sister when she was feeling sad.

Besides, thought AJ, *this turned out a lot better than that time we were coming home from Montana on a trip. Dad didn't stop the car in time.*

Recalling that horrible memory made AJ's stomach queasy.

The further they drove, the more convinced AJ became that they were going to visit her grandmother and Miranda. The only thing that bothered her was that they hadn't brought clothes to stay overnight. It was a long way to drive for a one-day visit.

It was around noon when her father pulled into her grandmother's driveway. "So we were going to St. George," AJ said to her parents. "Why didn't you tell us this morning that we were going to visit Grandma?"

"You'll see," answered her father.

Noticing a big rental truck parked in front of the house, AJ wondered what it was doing there. But before giving it any more thought, she hurried to find Grandma and Miranda.

As AJ raced into her grandmother's house, she was startled to see Jake and Josh, her twin brothers. "What are you guys doing here?" she asked. "And how did you get here?"

"Hi, everyone," Grandma called from the kitchen.

AJ ran to the kitchen. Everything was out of the cupboards, and Grandma's house was a wreck. "What are you doing, Grandma?" AJ asked bewildered. "Why is everything out of place?"

"Didn't your mom and dad tell you? I'm coming to live with you."

AJ's eyes widened with surprise. "Live with us?" she cried. "That'll be great!" AJ flung her arms around her grandmother.

The kitchen overflowed with excitement as the Bexton family gathered. "So that's why you wouldn't tell AJ and Sara and me where we were going," said Jen with a grin. "This is the surprise you had for us."

"And Jake and Josh drove the truck down to take Grandma's things back," said AJ, putting the puzzle together.

Just then a bustling mass of golden fur bounded into the kitchen. "Miranda!" AJ cried. "You and Grandma are coming to live with us." She grabbed her favorite dog. "I can't believe this is really happening."

"Oh, Miranda's not coming," said AJ's father. "It's just Grandma."

AJ's face sobered. "Why can't we take Miranda, too?" she asked. "We can't leave her here alone."

"I've found some neighbors who really want her," said Grandma. "Your father said that having a dog in your neighborhood would be difficult. And I have to agree with him. You don't have a fence or a doghouse. It probably wouldn't work."

"But we can build a fence," said AJ. "And we can build a doghouse. We can't go off and leave Miranda with someone else."

"I'm sorry, AJ," said her father. "We've already discussed this with Grandma and agreed that it's better to leave her with the neighbors."

"C'mon, Jake," said Josh. "Let's get Grandma's nightstand into the truck. We haven't got all day."

The family dispersed from the kitchen so they could pack Grandma's things. AJ and Grandma remained. "I just don't think it's fair," said AJ. "I could take good care of Miranda. Don't you feel terrible about leaving her?" she asked her grandmother.

"I really do," said Grandma. "But I think your father is right. It'd be hard to keep Miranda in your neighborhood. She might even run away."

Grandma slipped her arm around AJ. "Why don't you come and help me gather a few things together? I could use some help."

AJ pulled herself away from Miranda. She and Grandma walked into the bedroom. As they emptied some of the drawers, they overheard Jen and her mother talking.

"Mom," said Jen, "where's Grandma going to stay? I mean, which bedroom is she going to have?"

"I thought maybe you could move in with AJ," answered her mother.

"No way," said Jen. "I need my own room. How could you think of this without even asking me?"

AJ glanced at her grandmother, who was trying to act as though she didn't hear the conversation. AJ's heart quickened. She didn't want her grandmother to think she was causing trouble by coming.

"Why can't AJ move in with Sara and give Grandma her room?" asked Jen.

Tears filled Grandmother's eyes. AJ couldn't stand

to see her hurt like this. AJ burst into the hall. "I'd love to move in with Sara and let Grandma have my room," said AJ. "I think Grandma would like it better, anyway."

Jen's face flushed with embarrassment as she realized she had been overheard.

Grandma entered the hallway. "Maybe I could use Benj's room in the basement," she said. "I don't want you girls to move out of your rooms just for me."

AJ knew her grandmother was close to crying. "Sara's room is plenty big for both of us," said AJ. "Besides, if you move into my room, then I'll have you right next door to Sara and me."

AJ's mother interrupted, hoping to save further embarrassment to both Jen and Grandma. "I agree with you, AJ," she said. "Your room would be perfect for Grandma. I should've thought of that in the first place."

As AJ and Grandma went back into the bedroom to box a few more things, AJ couldn't help but think about moving in with Sara. Sara was so messy. And how would she ever study with Sara always in the room talking? She glanced at her grandmother.

So what! she thought. Maybe it'd be hard to be with Sara, but it would be great fun to have Grandma with them. She walked over and gave Grandma a hug. "I'm so glad you're coming with us," she said. "We're going to have a great time together."

AJ's dark brown eyes met Grandma's sky-blue ones. She and her grandmother were more than fifty years apart in age, but somehow they shared a deep connection.

Grandma smiled and continued to empty her drawer into a box. She turned away so AJ couldn't see her tears.

AJ's father was busy outside giving the boys directions on how to load the truck. "Be sure and wrap the small table with these blankets so it doesn't get scratched," he said. "Everything in the house that has a sheet over it is to be left," he added. "Grandma's renting her house to a family who needs to use her furniture."

After a quick, late lunch, Jake and Josh loaded the last small dresser into the truck. "Is it okay if we leave?" Jake asked. "It's going to take us some time to unload this when we get home."

"I'm going to go with the twins," said Jen. "I'll help them unload."

AJ's brothers and Jen waved as they pulled out of the driveway. "See you at home," called AJ's mother. "And be careful driving."

"Let's hurry and vacuum the house so we can leave, too," said AJ's father. "AJ, why don't you and Grandma take Miranda to the neighbors?"

AJ's heart sank. Could she really leave Miranda knowing that she might never see her again?

Borage—courage

2

An Unexpected Guest

"C'mere, Miranda," AJ called.

The large golden retriever bounded over to her. "Here, girl, let me put this leash on you," said AJ.

Miranda was excited to see the leash—that meant a walk. She looked eagerly into AJ's eyes and tried to lick her face.

"Hold still," said AJ. "I can't get this on you."

When the leash snapped shut, AJ hugged the excited dog. "If only you understood what is happening, you wouldn't be so happy," said AJ. She affectionately patted Miranda's head. "Are you ready, Grandma?" AJ called.

Together, Grandma and AJ walked Miranda down the street. Grandma motioned to a fenced, red-brick home. Two small children were playing in the yard. "This is where the Johnsons live," Grandma said. "And now, Miranda will live here too."

When they led Miranda into the yard, the children squealed with delight. Their parents soon appeared, and Grandmother introduced them to AJ.

"The children are so excited to have their own dog," said Mrs. Johnson. "I hope they're not too rough with her."

"Miranda's very good with children," Grandma assured her. "Keep her inside your fence, though, because she loves to run."

AJ knelt down beside Miranda and buried her face in the thick, golden fur. She was embarrassed to cry in front of the Johnsons, but she couldn't hold back the tears. Hugging Miranda made her want the dog more than ever. But she knew she must face reality. Standing up, she patted Miranda's head, wiped her eyes, and took Grandma's hand.

"We'd better go," AJ said bravely.

Miranda barked loudly as the gate clicked shut. AJ couldn't bear to turn and look at Miranda inside the fenced yard. She clutched Grandma's hand as Miranda's barking rang in her ears.

"I'll keep in touch," Grandma promised the Johnsons as she and AJ turned to leave.

Grandma and AJ had nearly reached Grandma's house when she turned to AJ. "Sometimes life is very difficult, AJ. This is one of those times. But I know you, and I know you'll be okay."

AJ looked into her grandmother's worn yet very wise face. She knew Grandma understood her feelings and the heartbreak she felt within.

Mom and Dad and Sara were already inside the Suburban.

"Just a moment," said Grandma. "I forgot something. I'll be right back."

Grandma hurried to the back of the house as though she intended to go inside. AJ watched as Grandmother stood and looked lovingly at her white frame home. Grandma was leaving not only Miranda but also the home where she had raised all of her children.

AJ walked quietly over to Grandma's side. "I love your home," AJ said. "We'll have to come back and visit, won't we?"

Now it was Grandma's turn to fight back the tears. AJ took hold of her hand and squeezed it. "I'm glad you're coming home with me," she said.

Both were especially quiet when they climbed into the Suburban for the long drive home.

"We've got to stop for gas," announced AJ's father as they pulled out of the driveway. "Everyone be thinking of a treat they'd like. Okay?"

AJ knew her father was trying to brighten the somber atmosphere. As they left Grandma's neighborhood, AJ glanced out the back window and caught a brief glimpse of the Johnson home. Miranda was barking loudly, as if she were telling them to wait for her. Tears trickled down AJ's cheeks.

Her father pulled into a gas station at the far end of town. "All right," he said as he stopped the car in front of the gas pump. "Everyone tell me what treat you want."

Sara eagerly gave her order, and AJ said she'd like a cold drink. It really didn't matter what kind.

AJ was lost in her thoughts about Miranda. What if the Johnsons were mean to her? What if they forgot to feed her and give her water? What if the little children pulled on her fur too hard? Could Miranda really be happy with them?

The questions loomed in AJ's mind. She still believed that she could find a way to care for Miranda, if only she had a chance.

AJ gazed out the window as she waited for her father to pay for the gas and treats. She thought she heard barking. *Must be some dogs around the gas station,* she thought. Then she blinked, almost afraid to believe what she was seeing.

Loping down the road was a blur of golden fur with a pink tongue hanging out.

"Grandma!" AJ shouted. "Miranda's coming!"

Sure enough. Miranda raced down the street toward the Suburban. AJ jumped out of the car and grabbed the panting dog. Miranda seemed to be grinning as she jumped up on AJ.

"The Johnsons must have left their gate open," said Grandma, crawling out of the car.

Sara squealed with delight as Miranda licked her face.

Just then, AJ's father walked out with his hands full of treats. His face betrayed his disbelief at spotting AJ hugging Miranda.

"Dad!" exclaimed AJ. "Can you believe she found us here?"

Her father stood speechless, shaking his head.

"Please, Dad," AJ pleaded, "please let me take her home with us."

3

Moving In

AJ's father shook his head. "That crazy dog wants to go with you as much as you want her to go. What do we do now?" he asked puzzled, looking at his wife for an answer.

"Oh, honey, let her come," grinned AJ's mother. "We'll figure out something to do with her."

"I'd better call the Johnsons and tell them they'll have to find another dog," said Grandma as she turned and winked at AJ.

"A dog!" squealed Sara. "We're going to have a dog!"

"Dad," said AJ, "are you sure it's okay with you? I mean, I know you didn't want her to come, and uh ..."

"It's just that we don't have a place for her," he said. "But I guess we'll find something."

AJ grabbed her father and hugged him hard. "I promise to take good care of her. I'll feed her and bathe her, and you won't even know she's around."

Her father took a deep breath, then turned to Grandma. "You'd better make that call so we can be on our way home."

"Yes!" exclaimed AJ, hugging Miranda. "We're *all* going home!"

The usual six-hour ride home took a little longer. Periodically, AJ had her father stop the car so she could take Miranda outside. But the ride still seemed to go quickly.

"Everybody! Help me unpack the Suburban," AJ's father called out as they pulled into their driveway. "It won't take us long if we all help."

Miranda leaped outside. She was tired of being cooped up and was eager to search out her new territory. She immediately headed for the bushes.

"No!" Dad yelled. "Not on that bush!" But it was too late. "AJ, you're going to have to put her on a rope and keep her out of the front yard. I don't want all of our bushes and flowers ruined."

AJ found a rope in the garage and tied Miranda to a tree in the backyard. She looked around. *Where are we going to put her?* AJ wondered. She felt a little uneasy, knowing how much her father liked to keep an immaculate yard.

"Now stay here, girl," AJ told Miranda. "And don't get into any trouble while I help unload the car."

Miranda barked. Her bark seemed much louder than it had in St. George. AJ rushed to help.

"Here, Grandma," said AJ. "Let me take these things to my room, I mean, to *your* room." AJ glanced at Grandma. "I guess it'll have to be *our* room until I can get my things out of there."

Grandma smiled as she followed AJ into the house.

Dropping her load of boxes on her bed, AJ turned to Grandma. "You're going to love this room. It has a big closet, and it's next door to the bathroom."

"Are you sure you don't mind moving out of here?" Grandma asked hesitantly. "Why don't we take these things to Benj's room in the basement? Then you can keep your room."

"Grandma, look at me," said AJ. "You've got to know I'm telling the truth. It'll be fun having you next door. And I know Sara will like my moving in with her because she still gets scared at night."

Before Grandma could object any further, AJ hurried and slid her desk out into the hall.

"Here's a place for your dresser. And as soon as we get my dresser unloaded and moved into the other room, you will have plenty of space for your nightstand."

AJ moved her desk into Sara's room. Then she hurried and emptied her closet. *This is kind of crowded,* she thought as she scrunched her clothes into Sara's closet. She quickly scooted Sara's dresser to the other side of the room so she could move her dresser in. Then she rushed to help Grandma.

Grandma placed a picture of her husband on the nightstand. "I love that picture of Grandpa," said AJ. "That's just the way I always think of him—happy and laughing."

"And that he was," mused Grandma. "You're really going to love *this* picture," Grandma laughed, handing another picture to AJ. "The neighbor boy took it of Miranda and me."

"Grandma! I love it!"

"It's yours!" exclaimed Grandma.

AJ hugged her grandmother. "Thanks a lot. I'll put it right in the middle of my desk."

Suddenly, they both heard Miranda barking loudly.

"AJ," called her father. "Come out here and quiet this dog. The neighbors will all be calling."

Miranda was twisted up in the rope and barking frantically to be freed.

"You silly dog," said AJ. "I think I'll tie you by the garage for a while."

But Miranda's plans differed. She wiggled free and took off down the road. "Miranda!" AJ shouted. "Come back here!"

AJ tore after the dog, and her father stood in the driveway shaking his head. "I knew we should have left that dog in St. George," he mumbled.

It was dark and getting chilly as AJ chased after Miranda. When Miranda stopped to dig up some flowers at the city park, AJ grabbed her collar. "Miranda," AJ scolded, "you've got to obey me, or Dad will never let you stay."

All the way back home, AJ wondered how she was going to keep Miranda out of trouble and at home. As she tied her dog to the bumper of the Suburban, she heard her mother calling everyone to come inside for a late snack before going to bed.

AJ was especially quiet at the table.

"AJ, what are we going to do with Miranda?" her father asked. "There is no way she'll stay tied up while you go to school. And we don't want her running through the house. Do you think we'd better build a dog run for her?"

"That'd be great, Dad, if you had the time to do it," said AJ.

"No choice," he answered.

It was late, and AJ could tell that her father was tired from the long day. She appreciated her brothers when they offered to help build the dog run after school on Monday.

That night as AJ crawled into bed, she couldn't help thinking about Miranda sleeping in the garage. It would be great for her to have a dog run so she could move around freely. Perhaps they could also build a doghouse to keep her warm in the winter. Everything seemed to be falling into place.

Suddenly, AJ heard a strange sound. She looked over at Sara, who was sound asleep. She heard it again. It sounded as if a little child was crying.

AJ slipped out of bed and crept down the stairs. The sound grew louder and louder. "Oh, no," whispered AJ. "It's coming from the garage."

By that time AJ reached the garage door, the strange sound had developed into a loud wail. "Miranda," AJ whispered through the door. "Be quiet and go to sleep. You're going to wake up Dad."

The forlorn wail escalated into a loud bark. Miranda was ecstatic to have a visitor. "Do you want me to stay here with you a while?" she asked Miranda, patting her head.

AJ found a blanket in the Suburban, and she and Miranda snuggled on the garage floor. Every time AJ thought Miranda must be asleep, her brown eyes popped open and her tail wagged. Eventually AJ fell asleep, only to be wakened with a wet tongue licking her face.

"Oh, no!" gasped AJ. "It's morning." She slipped quickly into the house and as quietly as possible managed to crawl into bed just as Sara was waking.

4

Miranda

AJ was glad church didn't begin until noon. She was tired and sore from trying to sleep on the cement in the garage. Not wanting to let anyone know she had slept there, she acted unusually cheerful.

"Hi, Grandma," she called, spotting Grandma in the hall. "Did you sleep well last night?"

Grandma walked over to AJ's bed and sat down. "I slept just fine. How did *you* sleep?" From her tone, AJ sensed that Grandma knew what had happened with Miranda.

Sara jumped out of bed and gave Grandma a hug on her way out of the door. AJ was glad to have Grandma alone. "You know, don't you?" she asked.

"I did hear some noises last night and wondered why Miranda suddenly quieted down," said Grandma. "AJ, you can't sleep out in the garage every night."

"But I didn't want Dad to hear her," said AJ. "I think she'll do better tonight. She just needs to get used to her new home."

Grandma laughed. "She's lucky to have you on her side. Not too many kids would sleep out in the garage all night and not complain."

That afternoon at church, AJ sat next to Emily in their Merrie Miss class. AJ thought how lucky they were to be best friends and be in the same ward. And to make matters even better, they had a teacher, Sister Day, whom they both loved.

"Girls," said Sister Day, "to fulfill one of our requirements for the Gospel in Action Award, we're going to do a service project. What are some of your ideas?"

One of the girls suggested making candy for the bishop. Another suggested visiting a rest home. Emily raised her hand.

"Why don't we do something nice for the widows in our ward?" she asked. "AJ's grandmother came to live with them this weekend, and she's a widow. I know you'd all enjoy meeting her because she's extra special."

AJ's face flushed a little. Emily was always thinking of other people. She had a knack for being aware of people's feelings, especially if they were new or sad or needed someone to talk with them.

"I didn't know your grandmother was coming to live with you, AJ," said Sister Day. "Emily does have a good idea, and it'd help your grandmother feel more a part of the ward if she got to know your friends. Does everyone agree on Emily's idea?"

The class was enthusiastic about the project. One of the girls raised her hand.

"We need to remember the other widows in the ward, too," she said. "There's Sister Doal and Sister Brecken."

"And there's Brother Gruen," added Sister Day. "He's all alone, too."

A moan sounded throughout the room.

"Girls," said Sister Day, "just because Brother Gruen is a little hard to get along with doesn't mean we should leave him out of our project."

"But I don't think he'd even want to see us," said AJ. "He lives only two houses away from my family, and he never even says hello or acts as if he knows us. I think he hates everybody and everything."

"Have you ever gone to talk with him?" asked Sister Day. "Maybe he's just lonely and needs a friend."

The girls laughed. They all knew "Grouchy Gruen" and made sure they stayed out of his way.

Emily sat quietly, lost in thought. Suddenly she raised her hand. "I think Sister Day is right. Brother Gruen's grouchy, but he does have beautiful flowers. Anyone who has such a beautiful yard as he does can't hate everything."

"When we all go to visit AJ's grandmother and the other widows, let's make some treats for him, too, and see how he acts," said one of the girls. "It couldn't do any harm."

"How about it, girls?" said Sister Day. "Should we try it?"

The class agreed to include Brother Gruen. They decided to meet at AJ's home on Thursday afternoon at four o'clock.

That night when AJ knelt beside her bed, she thanked Heavenly Father for her family, for Grandmother coming to live with them, for Miranda, for her big brother Benj who was on a mission, and for Emily and Sister Day. She knew Grandmother would love meeting her Merrie Miss class.

AJ fell asleep listening to Miranda occasionally wailing softly out in the garage.

Monday morning, after AJ had fed Miranda and tied her to the tree in the backyard, Emily and AJ walked to school. They chatted about the upcoming service project. When they passed by Mr. Gruen's house, AJ cringed inside. She knew Grandmother would enjoy the project, but she had doubts about Mr. Gruen.

"He sure does have beautiful flowers," said Emily as they walked by.

Miss Bleezer was at her desk when they entered the school room. Ever since the writing contest in which Emily and AJ had won first and second places, Miss Bleezer had seemed to take more notice of them. She also increased the number of writing assignments each week.

"This morning, class, we're going to begin this week by introducing an interesting writing project," announced Miss Bleezer.

The students groaned, but she paid no attention.

"Do any of you own a pet?" she asked. Nearly every student raised their hand.

"For all of those who don't," Miss Bleezer continued, "you can still do this assignment. I want you to spend time with a tame animal and try to communicate with it. On Thursday, I'll give you time in class to write about your communicating skills with your particular animal. Take notes on how they react to you, how much they understand you, and anything else that shows you are communicating with them. On Friday you'll hand in the final paper."

AJ grinned. *This will be an easy assignment,* she thought. *All I'll have to do is spend time with Miranda. It's easy to communicate with her.*

As soon as school was over, AJ was excited to get home, see Grandmother, and play with Miranda. She hurried into the backyard but stopped suddenly. What had happened to their yard!

There were big, ugly mounds of dirt on her father's groomed lawn, and flowers were lying all over. AJ gasped. The tree where she had tied Miranda still had the leash around it, but no dog was attached.

Her only hope was that Miranda was with Grandmother. She rushed into the house. "Grandma," she called, "is Miranda with you?"

Grandma was in the living room mending some of the boys' socks. "Hi, AJ," she called. "No, honey, Miranda's still out in the yard."

AJ's heart raced. She tore out the back door. *I've got to find her quick,* thought AJ. *And somehow I've got to fix up the yard before Dad gets home.*

AJ ran down the street calling for Miranda. As she neared Mr. Gruen's house, she stopped dead in her tracks. In the middle of Mr. Gruen's flower bed, Miranda was busily digging a hole, her tail wagging. When she spied AJ, she romped over to her and jumped on her, leaving dirty footprints on AJ's shirt.

Before AJ knew what to do, she heard someone yelling.

"Who did this to my flowers?" demanded Mr. Gruen. He stalked out to the front yard where AJ was standing. The tell-tale dirt on Miranda explained the mess in his flowers. Mr. Gruen's face purpled with rage, and he shook his fist at AJ.

"Y-y-y-your d-dog," he stammered angrily, "h-has ruined my flowers!"

"I'm sorry," said AJ, not knowing what else to say. "I didn't know she was in your yard until now and—"

"I'm calling the police!" shouted Mr. Gruen. "You'll pay for this."

AJ ran up to the angry old man. "I'm really sorry," she said. "I didn't know my dog would do this, and I just got home from school. I promise she'll never do this again. Please, please don't call the police."

Mr. Gruen stared angrily at AJ and Miranda, turned, and stomped over to his wilted flowers lying in the dirt. "Get out of here!" he yelled. "And take that mangy dog with you."

AJ grabbed Miranda.

"Don't you ever come back," AJ heard Mr. Gruen shout as she hurried toward her house.

Once in her yard, she sat down with Miranda facing her. "Why did you do that, Miranda? Why did you ruin Dad's lawn and Mr. Gruen's flowers?"

Miranda looked puzzled. She wagged her tail and licked AJ's face.

"You silly old dog," bemoaned AJ. "You don't even know why I'm mad at you."

AJ locked Miranda in the garage and began the futile job of repairing her Dad's lawn.

"Hi, honey," Mom called from the kitchen. "When did you get home from school? And what are you doing?"

As her mother walked into the yard, she gasped. "Oh, AJ, what's happened to our yard?"

AJ kept her head down as she tried to fill in one of the holes with dirt and cover it over with sod. "Dad will kill Miranda if he sees this, Mom. I've got to clean this up before he gets home."

Grandmother joined them in the yard. She knew

immediately what had happened. Without saying a word, she motioned to AJ's mother to join her as she knelt down and started filling in one of the holes.

"I'm sorry, AJ," said Grandma. "Maybe we should've left Miranda in St. George."

By the time AJ's father arrived home from work, the yard had been repaired as much as possible. AJ hoped her father wouldn't go outside.

That night at dinner AJ was extra quiet.

"AJ," said her father after a few minutes, "I happened to walk out in our yard before dinner. Is there something you'd like to tell me?"

AJ looked up at her dad. Before she could say anything, the doorbell rang. AJ's heart sank as her father opened the door and she saw a policeman standing on the porch.

Carnation—a woman's love, motherly love

5

Mending Holes

Mr. Bexton invited the policeman inside. After listening to the complaint filed against Miranda by Mr. Gruen, her dad looked disgustedly at AJ.

"Did Mr. Gruen file any financial charges?" he asked the policeman.

"No, he said he decided to drop those. But he was pretty mad. Just make sure your dog doesn't dig up the old man's yard again," the policeman added. "The next time I'll have to take her in."

AJ looked at her father. "I'm sorry, Dad," she said. "I had no idea Miranda would cause all this trouble."

"Guess we'd better get started on a fence," her father said.

The policeman turned to leave.

"Thanks for coming over," AJ's father said. "Sorry to cause you trouble."

"C'mon, AJ," said Jake, putting his arm around his little sister. "Josh and I will help Dad tonight. It won't take us very long to put up some kind of fence to keep Miranda in."

"I had planned the lesson for family home evening," said her mother, "but I think we'll do a family fence project instead. We'll clear up all the dishes while you men go to the lumberyard and pick up materials."

Jen looked disgusted. "I don't have time to build a dumb fence," she moaned.

AJ knew her big sister was irritated with all the problems Miranda had caused. "That's okay," said AJ. "I can help Dad."

At ten-thirty that night AJ was still pounding nails. "Let's have our family prayer," said AJ's mother. "The kids have to get to bed. It's school tomorrow."

"All right," agreed her husband. The weary group made their way into the family room. Grandma had glasses of lemonade waiting.

As they knelt that night, AJ looked around at her father, mother, grandmother, brothers, and sisters. "Thanks for putting up the fence tonight," said AJ. Tears welled up in her eyes. "I never dreamed Miranda would be so much trouble. I guess we should have left her in St. George with the Johnsons."

Her father grinned. "She sure did cause a lot of trouble today. But just remember, AJ, loving something or someone doesn't always mean it's going to be easy. But if you really love them, the work will be worth it."

He hugged AJ and asked her to say the family prayer.

It was well past eleven when AJ snuggled into her bed. She fell asleep hearing the tapping of her father's hammer. She thought she heard Miranda barking, but she fell asleep hoping it was just a bad dream.

First thing in the morning AJ jumped out of bed and raced to the window to see the new fence. To her dismay, it wasn't quite finished. She decided to keep Miranda in the garage instead of tying her to the tree. She'd have Grandma watch her during the day while she was at school.

When Emily met AJ to walk to school that morning, AJ told her all about the horrible incident with Mr. Gruen's flowers.

"She really did mess up his flowers!" exclaimed Emily as they passed Mr. Gruen's place. "Weren't you scared when he came out to see this?"

"I was scared to death," admitted AJ. "He yelled at me and told me to keep Miranda away from his yard. Then he sent a policeman over to our house."

Emily's eyes widened with interest. "Did he make you pay for new flowers?"

"No," answered AJ. "He just sent the policeman to warn us to keep Miranda away."

"Maybe you can use some of this in your report on communicating with animals," said Emily.

"I doubt it," said AJ. "Miranda and I haven't communicated very well at all. Guess I'll have to work on that this afternoon when we get home from school. But, most important, I'm going to help my dad finish the fence."

"Do you think Miranda will understand why she has to stay inside the fence?" Emily asked. "I mean, do you think she realizes she's done anything wrong?"

"I don't think so," said AJ. "When we were assigned to communicate with an animal, I thought it'd be easy. I planned to spend time with Miranda and write about how well we understood each other. But from what's happened, I don't think she understands me at all—other than she knows I love her."

Emily laughed. "That's what's happened with my cat. When I started paying close attention to what I said to her and how she reacted to me, I was surprised. I'd always thought she'd understood what I said. But what I discovered was that she was more concerned about being fed."

"I know what you mean," said AJ. "Miranda surely doesn't understand what I say. When I scolded her for digging up Mr. Gruen's flowers, she licked my face."

"Do you think he's still mad?" Emily asked.

"Probably," answered AJ. "The only thing I really dread is going to his place with our Merrie Miss class. I hope he doesn't yell at me again."

Emily turned up the street toward her home. "Good luck on writing your paper tonight. See you in the morning."

"Hi, AJ," Grandma called as AJ opened the front door. "You'll never believe what a good dog Miranda's been today. She hasn't barked all afternoon, and she's not even tried to jump over the fence."

AJ grinned. Grandmother always knew how to brighten her day.

"Let's go outside and give her a bone," suggested Grandma. "I think she misses you during the day."

AJ and Grandma opened the gate, and Miranda excitedly wagged her tail and jumped up on AJ.

As AJ patted her head and hugged her, she turned to her grandmother.

"I'm writing a paper about Miranda for English," said AJ.

"Is that so?"

"You won't believe it, but it's on how well I communicate with her. I thought that'd be easy. But I don't think Miranda understands one thing I say. She never has figured out why I scolded her for digging up Mr. Gruen's flowers."

"That's the way animals are," said Grandma. "Miranda's a smart dog. But animals don't have the ability to reason. They go by their instincts. She knows when she's hungry, when you're happy, and when you want to be quiet and pet her instead of playing ball with her. But she can't reason. All she knows is that digging up those flowers was fun. It was a game—a digging game. Dogs have an instinct to dig, like when they bury their bones."

"But not all dogs go around digging up flowers," said AJ. "And what about the dogs who obey their masters' commands? They seem to know right from wrong."

"That's why people send their dogs to obedience school," said Grandma. "They're taught to obey commands. But they still go a lot by their instincts. Animals know when someone loves them, just like Miranda knows that you love her a great deal. Dogs know when someone is afraid of them. That's why dogs chase you if you run away from them in fear."

"I know one thing for sure," said AJ. "Having a pet doesn't mean living happily ever after."

Grandma laughed. "Maybe not happily ever after, but having a pet can be the beginning of many fun adventures."

"That's it!" exclaimed AJ. "I'll use that for the title of my paper. 'The Beginning of Many Fun Adventures.'"

That night as AJ wrote her paper, she was glad Grandma had talked with her. She felt that she understood Miranda better and perhaps wouldn't expect things of Miranda now that weren't possible for her to understand.

On Thursday afternoon, AJ's Merrie Miss class was at her home visiting with her grandmother. Grandma was excited to meet the girls, and they certainly enjoyed her.

"Sister Day," said Grandma, "I think you have the best calling in the ward as Merrie Miss teacher."

"I agree," said Sister Day. "Especially in this ward, because these girls are really special. And now we're off to visit a couple of other people in our ward."

"Does that mean going to Brother Gruen's?" asked one of the girls.

"Who is this Brother Gruen?" asked Grandma as she heard the girls moaning.

"Remember, Grandma?" said AJ. "He's our neighbor who sent the policeman to our house because Miranda dug up his flowers."

"Oh, that Brother Gruen," said Grandma. "I understand not too many people around here like him."

"He's rather grouchy," said Sister Day, "so people stay away from him. We really don't know him very well."

"Why don't you come with us, Grandma," said AJ. "You like everybody—maybe when Brother Gruen meets you, he'll let us visit him."

"That's a great idea!" said Sister Day. "That is, if it's okay with your grandmother."

Grandma put a sweater around her shoulders, and they all headed for Brother Gruen's home.

The girls rang the doorbell three times. They were startled when they heard a muffled voice telling them to go away.

"We came to visit you," called Grandma through the closed door. "We even have a plate of chocolate chip cookies for you."

It must have been the charm of Grandma's voice that enticed the old man to open the door. He looked surprised when he saw all the girls, Sister Day, and Grandma bunched on his front porch.

"Hello, Brother Gruen," said Sister Day. "We're the Merrie Miss class from the ward, and we wanted to visit with you and bring you these cookies." She handed Brother Gruen the plate.

Brother Gruen looked suspiciously at the cookies and then at the girls. Then he caught sight of Grandma.

"I'm your new neighbor," said Grandma. "This is my granddaughter, AJ. I think you know her."

The old man's eyes winced as he recognized AJ. But before he could say anything to dampen the group's cheerfulness, Grandma walked over to his side.

"Brother Gruen, these are the sweetest girls you'll ever meet. I think you should know each one of their names so you can say hello to them at church."

Before he could protest, Grandma introduced each girl and had her tell Brother Gruen where she lived.

"Now we've got to be getting along," said Grandma as she noticed Mr. Gruen getting a little uneasy. "You be sure and enjoy those wonderful cookies. And be sure and come to church on Sunday so we can all visit with you."

With that, Grandma and the Merrie Miss girls waved good-bye and were on their way, leaving one surprised old man standing on his porch holding a plate of cookies.

When the group was out of Mr. Gruen's sight, Sister Day turned to Grandma. "Why, you're an angel!" she exclaimed. "Never could we have said what you said to Brother Gruen and got away with it. You had him spellbound."

AJ laughed. "That's my grandma," she said. "Whenever you want something done and done right, ask her."

"Brother Gruen's not been to church in months," said Emily. "It'll be interesting to see if he comes on Sunday."

"Would you like to come with us to the other widows in the ward?" asked Sister Day. "I'll bet you'd like to meet them, and I know they'd sure like to meet you."

The girls swarmed around Grandma as AJ took hold of her arm. What a sight as they walked through the neighborhood giggling and laughing!

"You sure made a hit with my Merrie Miss class," AJ told Grandma that evening as they sat at the kitchen counter. AJ was rewriting her English paper, and Grandma was darning holes in Jake's socks.

"I can still see the shock on Brother Gruen's face when you introduced all of us girls to him and told him you hoped to see him at church," said AJ, laughing. "He's probably still in shock."

Grandmother chuckled. "Old people are a lot like old socks, AJ. They become old and worn out and full of holes. But that doesn't mean there's no more use for them. For example, look at Jake's old socks." She held up Jake's sock and poked her fingers through the holes. "If you darn up these holes, there's a lot more wear in them. You just have to take the time to do some mending. I think you and Miranda are the ones to darn the holes in old Brother Gruen."

AJ stopped writing. "What do you mean, Grandma?" asked AJ. "How could Miranda and I do any good with an old man who is so ornery and grouchy?"

Grandmother smiled. "You'll think of something. There's a lot of ways to mend lonely feelings."

Aster—dainty, elegant

6

In the Dog Run

"I'm glad it's Friday," said AJ as she and Emily walked home from school.

"So am I," Emily agreed. "What are you doing this weekend?"

"We still need to build a doghouse for Miranda," said AJ. "I'll be helping Dad with that and just spending time with Miranda. She still barks at night and isn't used to her fenced dog run. What are you doing?"

"Just some homework," replied Emily. She was extra quiet.

"If you need a break, come over and help me build," AJ said as she and Emily parted at the corner. As AJ walked home, she wondered what was bothering her best friend.

That evening, AJ's parents were at a movie, Jen was with her friends, the twins were at the ward meetinghouse playing basketball, and Sara was at a birthday party. AJ and Grandma sat on the back porch watching Miranda play with a ball.

"How did your report on Miranda turn out?" asked Grandma.

"I handed it in today. Actually, it was kind of fun to write," said AJ. "It made me realize that I didn't understand her very well. But I think she knows I love her, just like you said. When I walk into the yard and she starts barking and wagging her tail, I feel she loves me, too."

Miranda bounced over to AJ and licked her cheek. "I've been thinking a lot about how you said Miranda and I could mend some of Brother Gruen's bad ways."

"Now, just a minute," interrupted Grandma, "I didn't say 'bad' ways. I said he had some holes that needed mending. I didn't mean to imply that he was bad."

"Why do you think he's so grouchy?" asked AJ.

"Perhaps he's lonely," said Grandma. "When people grow old, often no one seems to need them."

"But you don't feel that way, do you?" AJ asked.

"I'm lucky to have my family," said Grandma. "But even I have feelings like that sometimes. Old age is frustrating. After living so long, you want to share your ideas, but everyone's too busy to listen. Everyone needs to feel needed and appreciated."

"How could I make Brother Gruen feel needed?" asked AJ.

"If you could get him to talk, I'll bet he's got some fascinating stories," said Grandma. "And despite what you might think, he's probably got some fun left in those old bones."

"I doubt it," said AJ. "I can't imagine him laughing."

"That's the problem," said Grandma. "You see his bald head, wrinkles, and frown. Next time you're around him, imagine him with a head of dark brown hair and skin like yours. I promise, you'll feel differently toward him."

AJ laughed. "What you want me to do is think of him as being young so I don't treat him like he's old. Right?"

Grandma nodded.

"What's that sound?" asked AJ. "Do you hear that?"

Even Miranda sat still with her ears perked.

"I think someone is playing a flute or something," said Grandma.

The three of them listened intently in the direction of the music.

"It's a harmonica," said Grandmother. "Someone is playing a harmonica."

Miranda tilted her head back and joined in the melodious tune.

"Stop that, Miranda," said AJ, putting her hand over Miranda's mouth. "You'll bother the neighbors howling like that."

Miranda took no heed. She scooted away from AJ, tilted her head high in the air, and continued her duet with the harmonica. Grandma chuckled, and AJ knew it was no use trying to quiet Miranda.

Grandma and AJ laughed and laughed as they watched Miranda howl at the top of her lungs. As soon as the music stopped, she jumped up and bounced off in the direction of the music.

"Come back here, Miranda," shouted AJ. "Don't go running away."

"C'mere, Miranda," called Grandma, but to no avail. Miranda was off down the street.

"Let's go get her," AJ called to Grandma, and off they rushed.

Suddenly Miranda stopped and her ears perked up again—right in front of Brother Gruen's house!

"The music's coming from Brother Gruen's backyard," said AJ. "He must be the one playing the harmonica."

Miranda started howling again. Grandmother and AJ were stumped as to what to do.

The music stopped and a dark shadow appeared at the back gate. "Get that mangy dog out of here! Can't a person even enjoy his own music without being bothered?"

AJ recognized Brother Gruen's voice.

Miranda jumped toward the gate, tail wagging. "Get out of here, you mutt," he said, throwing a rock at Miranda. "All of you, get out of here."

"Here, Miranda," said Grandma in a low voice. "C'mon girl, let's go home."

She took hold of Miranda's collar and with AJ's help led her down the street.

"He really is something," said Grandma. "I've not met anyone else quite like him."

"Now can you understand why I don't want to ever go to his place?" asked AJ. "I think he hates everybody."

"All the more reason to find a way to do something nice for him," said Grandmother. "Anyone who's as mean and angry as he is needs lots of love and understanding."

Back home, AJ led Miranda to the fenced dog run.

"I think I'll stay out here for a while with Miranda," said AJ. "I think she gets lonely, and it's warm enough I don't even need a sweater."

"You're right. I think she does get lonely. Do you mind if I join the two of you?"

They locked the gate to the dog run so they wouldn't have to chase Miranda again. Both AJ and Grandma sat on the hard ground, and Miranda seemed delighted to have their company.

AJ laughed. "Grandma, do you know how ridiculous we look?"

Grandmother started laughing, too. "Quite a sight—the three of us locked up inside the dog pen."

They laughed even harder and Miranda barked.

"I never imagined us sitting inside a pen taking care of Miranda," chuckled AJ. "I thought when we brought her here from St. George, everything would be perfect."

Grandma's eyes twinkled. "I still can see the look on your face when Miranda dug up your father's lawn."

"And then when you and Mom were trying to help me flatten out all those mounds of dirt." AJ was laughing so hard her sides hurt. "I never thought I'd be able to laugh about that."

AJ became a little more serious. Looking into her Grandma's eyes, she said, "Even with all the troubles she's caused, I'm still glad she's here. And I'm glad you're here."

"I wish Jen felt that way," said Grandma. "I'm afraid I've become quite a bother to her."

AJ looked surprised. "Jen's never said anything to me," said AJ.

"Nor to me," said Grandma. "But I get in her way. Just like this morning when I came out of the bathroom. I didn't know Jen was waiting to shower. She had to be to school early, and I could tell she was upset."

"Jen's like that," said AJ. "She gets mad easily, but she forgives easily, too. I'm sure she's forgotten all about it."

"I don't want to cause any problems," said Grandma.

"My Merrie Miss class loves you. They all want to come and visit you again," said AJ. "Emily said I'm lucky to have a grandma like you. She said her grandmother is really quiet, and they don't ever do much together."

"Well, her grandmother is missing out by not spending more time with Emily, because she's a special girl," said Grandma. "The only way you get to really know someone is to spend time with them. That's how you build memories together."

"Grandma, I've got something to tell you that I've never told anyone else." Grandma and AJ scooted closer together.

"Remember when you gave me that pair of Grandpa's *lucky* suspenders?"

Grandma nodded.

"Well, I entered a writing contest, and when I wrote my paper I always had those suspenders on my desk, hoping they'd bring me good luck."

"And did they?"

"Not at first. My teacher lost my paper, and I had to write it again," replied AJ. "But this is the part you won't believe, Grandma. On the night the winners were to be announced, I *wore those suspenders under my dress!*"

"And did you win?" asked Grandma.

"I won second place."

"I love those suspenders, Grandma. They bring back so many happy memories of Grandpa. I'll bet you miss him terribly, don't you?"

"I sure do," answered Grandma. "Sometimes I look at the zillions of stars up there and wonder if he's watching. It'll be good to see him someday. At least I know we'll be together then."

"I wonder if Brother Gruen was ever married," mused AJ. "I've never seen anyone visiting him."

"Perhaps that's where you begin mending," said Grandma. "People who don't have a family to love them can have some mighty big holes inside."

Suddenly Miranda's fur bristled and she growled. "What is it, Miranda? What do you hear?" asked AJ.

AJ heard a rustling of leaves. "Grandma, someone's in our yard!"

Damask Rose—ambassador of love

7

"Grouchy Gruen"

Both AJ and Grandma scrambled to their feet. "Perhaps it's just another dog or cat," suggested Grandma.

"I don't think so, or Miranda wouldn't be growling," said AJ.

They heard footsteps running around the corner of the house.

"Grandma, someone is out there! What should we do?"

"Probably nothing now," said Grandma. "I think the intruder heard us and decided it was time to leave. Let's get Miranda settled down, and then I think it's time for us to go inside."

AJ made sure she locked the gate to Miranda's pen. She was glad that Grandma was home with her.

Early next morning, AJ was out in her backyard with her father and brothers, building a doghouse.

She could smell cinnamon rolls baking in the kitchen and knew that Grandma and Mom were busy, also. Sara came out occasionally to bring something to drink or snack.

All morning AJ's thoughts had been on her terrible old neighbor, "Grouchy Gruen."

"Well, it's almost time for lunch," said her father, wiping his brow. "AJ, you seem to have a lot on your mind this morning."

She looked at her father in his jeans and sweatshirt. She thought how much she liked him dressed like that. Usually he was in a suit and tie, which was okay. But she enjoyed his being this way, in the yard with her.

"All morning I've been thinking about something Grandma told me last night," said AJ. "She thinks I should do something nice for Brother Gruen."

"That's probably a good idea," said her father. "As I smell those cinnamon rolls, I don't know of a man on earth who could resist liking them."

"That's a great idea, Dad!" exclaimed AJ. "Miranda and I'll take him a plate of those for his lunch."

AJ dashed into the kitchen. "Mom, may I have some of your cinnamon rolls to give to Brother Gruen? Miranda and I'll take them down now so he can have them for lunch."

"Of course," said her mother. "We've got plenty. I just frosted these warm ones."

AJ washed her hands and combed her hair. She was a little nervous, yet excited to try this idea on her neighbor. Grandma walked into her room just as AJ snapped a bow into her hair.

"I heard about your idea," she said. "Good luck. How do you feel inside?"

"Kind of nervous," admitted AJ. "But I'm excited to see if this works. Do you want to come with me?"

"No," answered Grandma. "I think it's better for me to stay here. This is *your* mending project."

Grandma watched AJ and Miranda head up the street. "I sure hope this works," she whispered to herself.

AJ stopped in front of Brother Gruen's house. Her stomach growled and she felt a little sick. But she took a deep breath and looked at Miranda. "Now you be a good dog and don't jump up on him, okay?"

Miranda wagged her tail and looked at the rolls.

"I know, girl, you wish these were for you. Now be a good dog."

They both walked up to the front door, and AJ rang the doorbell.

They stood waiting. AJ started feeling really sick inside. "Maybe he's not home," she said to Miranda. "Maybe we should come back another day."

Suddenly the door opened. Facing AJ and Miranda was Brother Gruen, and he didn't look very happy to see them.

"W-we brought you some cinnamon rolls for your lunch," stammered AJ. "My mom made them. I thought you'd like some."

Whether it was the aroma of the cinnamon rolls or the shock of seeing AJ and Miranda at his doorstep, the old man didn't slam the door. He grunted something under his breath and motioned for both of them to come inside.

AJ placed the rolls on his kitchen table. She looked around and thought how dreary his home looked. The curtains were all drawn, and the house felt dark and gloomy. There were a few dirty dishes in the sink, and newspapers were strewn on the floor.

"Well, sit down if you want," said Brother Gruen gruffly.

"Oh, no, we have to be going," AJ replied. "We just wanted to come and bring this treat."

"There must be something you want!" demanded the old man. "No one just goes around taking dessert to people."

"Honest, that's the only reason we came," said AJ.

She motioned to Miranda. "C'mon, girl. Let's go home."

"No, wait," growled the old man. "Why don't you have one of these rolls with me?"

As Mr. Gruen removed the plastic wrap covering the rolls, Miranda wagged her tail excitedly. AJ was busy studying him. She recalled Grandma's advice to think of brown hair and no wrinkles. For a moment, she imagined an entirely different person at the table. He handed a roll to AJ.

"Thanks," said AJ politely. "I think you'll like these. My dad says no one can resist them."

"So, you want to know if I was ever married?" asked the old man. AJ's face flushed with embarrassment.

"How did you know I wanted to know if you were married?" she asked. "The only person I ever said that to was my grandmother, and that was—"

Brother Gruen nervously picked up a roll. "Never mind. It's not important," he said, trying to change the subject.

"But it is important," protested AJ. "The only way

you could know that I had said that is for you to have been in our yard last night. So, you were the one!"

"I was not!" he argued.

"Why were you snooping in our yard?" demanded AJ.

"I wasn't snooping," he sneered. "I was just out taking a walk and—"

"And you came into our yard and listened to what Grandma and I were saying," interrupted AJ. "I can't believe you'd do a thing like that."

"I wasn't doing anything wrong," he grumbled.

"But you frightened us," said AJ. "Why didn't you let us know who you were when Miranda started barking?"

"You had no right to be talking about me," he growled. "My personal life is none of your business. And how do you know that no one ever visits me? Are you always watching my place?"

AJ felt her temper rising at the old man. "No, I don't watch your place. I just told my grandmother that I'd never seen anyone coming here to visit you."

AJ turned to go. "C'mon, Miranda. Let's go home."

Brother Gruen grabbed the rolls off the table. "Here, take the rest of these," he grumbled.

Miranda couldn't resist the temptation. She leaped in the air to grasp the plate of still-warm cinnamon rolls. Brother Gruen and the rolls crashed to the floor.

Brother Gruen was shocked! "Get your dog off me!" he yelled. "She's going to kill me!"

"C'mere, Miranda," pleaded AJ. "Get off Brother Gruen and let's go home."

But Miranda stood over the fuming man while she gulped the rolls. Finally, she licked the plate and ran out the door, which AJ was holding open. Brother Gruen pulled himself up and shook his fist at Miranda.

"Your dog's a monster," he shouted at AJ. "It attacked me!"

AJ knew it was no use to argue with her stubborn neighbor. She raced out the door and down the street toward home with Miranda close behind her. She heard the old man yelling after them.

"I'm calling the police!" he shouted.

AJ's heart pounded as she tore through her front door. Bursting into tears, she ran into Grandma's room, Miranda at her heels.

"What on earth happened?" asked her grandmother.

"Grandma, he's going to call the police! Miranda jumped on him."

"She jumped on him!" exclaimed her father rushing to the scene. "What got into that dog?"

AJ sobbed. "She wanted one of the cinnamon rolls. When she jumped up to get it, she knocked Brother Gruen to the floor."

"All right," said her father, trying to calm AJ down. By now everyone in the family was gathered in Grandma's room, surrounding AJ. "Let's all settle down, and you can tell us exactly what happened."

AJ wiped her tears and took a couple of deep breaths. She explained the incident in detail. "I hate him," she said. "Miranda and I wanted to do something nice for him. But he doesn't want anyone to be good to him. Now the police will come and take Miranda."

It wasn't long before the doorbell rang. The dog catcher and a policeman were standing at the door. Miranda raced to greet them, licking their hands and wagging her tail.

"Is this the dog who attacked Mr. Gruen?" the policeman asked incredulously.

"She's the one," said AJ's father, motioning for them to come inside. "I'm afraid we've got a real problem on our hands," he said. "Our daughter just told us what happened, and I think it'd be good for you to know the story also."

After hearing AJ's story, the policeman shook his head. "That's too bad it turned out the way it did. But I do have to take your dog in. Mr. Gruen demanded that she be taken in for a ten-day quarantine to be checked for rabies."

"She doesn't have rabies," AJ interrupted.

"I'm sure she's all right," said the dog catcher. "We'll take good care of her. In the meantime, it'd help if you could find a way to make amends with your neighbor. He's pretty upset."

The dog catcher snapped a leash on Miranda and led her to the truck. The policeman was still talking with AJ's father and writing down the details. AJ stood at the front door with Grandma at her side.

"It sure doesn't help to do nice things for some people, does it?" AJ said quietly. "I wish I'd never gone to see that old man."

Grandma didn't say a word; she just put her arm around AJ's shoulders. Tears trickled down AJ's cheeks as she watched the dog catcher slam the door on his truck. Miranda barked, scratching to get out. She was still barking and scratching as the truck pulled away.

8

Sister Day's Challenge

"Why were the police at your home last night?" Emily asked AJ as they walked to Merrie Miss class on Sunday. "I was out in the yard and saw a police car and the dog catcher's truck pull up in the front of your home."

"Em, you'll never believe what happened," said AJ quietly. "They took Miranda away for ten days."

Emily was shocked. Before she could ask more questions, Sister Day walked into their classroom. "Hello, girls," she said cheerfully. "I'm glad you're all here today."

After an opening prayer, Sister Day asked, "Did you all have a good time on our service project this week?"

"That was lots of fun," said one of the girls. "I think AJ has a really neat grandma."

AJ was surprised that Emily didn't say anything

about her grandmother. Emily was usually the first to say nice things about people.

"And what about Brother Gruen?" Sister Day asked. "Did he come to church today?"

No one had seen him.

"I doubt if he'll come," said AJ. "I had a terrible experience with him yesterday."

The class quieted. They listened intently as AJ told about her grandmother's idea of "mending the holes" in Brother Gruen. Then she explained about taking the cinnamon rolls and the fiasco of her visit.

Sister Day sat quietly, listening to every word.

"That's why I don't think he'll ever come to church," said AJ. "And I don't care. I really don't like him."

"He is an ornery old man," agreed Sister Day. "But I wouldn't give up yet, AJ. I think your grandmother is right. For someone to be so angry at the world, he must be carrying a heavy burden."

"Did your grandmother try to see him after Miranda knocked him down?" one of the girls asked. "She seems to be able to make anyone listen."

"No," answered AJ. "But I don't think Brother Gruen will listen to anyone right now. He's really mad."

"What are you going to do, AJ?" Sister Day asked. "Have you any plans for befriending him?"

"Not really," replied AJ. "Actually, I don't know if I want to be nice to him. He's so mean."

"I know about a person who was in a situation much like yours, AJ," said Sister Day.

The Merrie Miss girls were quiet as they anticipated Sister Day's story.

"Many years ago, there was a man who lived across the ocean. He walked around the countryside telling people stories about how they could live happier lives. He was kind and loving, and those who took the time to listen to his stories knew that he was a very special person.

"But there were others who wouldn't listen. They hated him. Perhaps it was because their hearts were full of anger and bad feelings.

"Some people hated him so badly that they made fun of him and tried to trick him into doing or saying things that would get him in trouble. But that didn't stop him from doing good.

"He told the people many stories when he was teaching them. One story he told was about a shepherd who had one hundred sheep. He knew them all by name because he loved them. One evening as he gathered his sheep, one of them was missing. It might have been cold and dark, but the shepherd searched and searched until he finally found the one lost sheep. He put him over his shoulders and carried him home, rejoicing. When he arrived home, he called his friends and neighbors and asked them to celebrate with him, for he had found his sheep that was lost.

"Now, the people might have been thinking of sheep, but the master storyteller continued. He said that we are all his sheep. Some of us might become lost. We might lose our way. But great is the joy in heaven when those who have sinned or strayed away are brought back to the fold."

Some of the girls in the class looked at each other and whispered that they knew who this story was about. Sister Day continued:

"Hate can do terrible things to a person's judgment. The hateful people became enraged at the goodness of this man. They spit on him, made fun of him, and eventually had him put to death on a cross.

"You know who this is about, don't you?" Sister Day said. "And you're right. It's about the Savior. But the stories he taught the people so many years ago still apply in our day. As long as people have lived on earth, there has been hate and love. The Savior told us to love. He admonished us to search after his lost sheep and bring them back to the fold.

"I know this might sound silly, AJ, but in this same kind of situation, what do you think the Savior would tell you to do?" asked Sister Day.

AJ sat quietly and finally said, "He'd tell me to love Brother Gruen."

"But how can AJ love Brother Gruen when he won't even try to be nice?" Emily asked.

"Let me tell just one more story," said Sister Day. "One day the Savior went up into a mountain, and his disciples were around him. People had gathered from far and near to hear his message. This is when he gave the Sermon on the Mount. I'm sure you remember part of it, such a 'Blessed are the poor in spirit: for theirs is the kingdom of heaven.'"

The girls nodded.

"He also taught the multitude about people who hate them. He told the people to love their enemies, to bless those who cursed them, and to do good to those who hated them. He also told the people, 'Pray for them which despitefully use you, and persecute you.'"

Sister Day looked at the girls. "Think of the

words, 'despitefully use you, and persecute you.' That means being unfair with you, being mean to you, and doing things which hurt you."

"Just like the way Brother Gruen is with AJ," said Emily.

"A lot like that," agreed Sister Day. "And what are we supposed to do for them?"

"Pray for them," said one of the girls.

"Do you think you could pray for your enemy?" Sister Day asked.

"I never thought of Brother Gruen as my enemy, but I guess that's what he is," said AJ. "He certainly isn't my friend. But I don't know if I could ever pray for him. It's hard to pray for someone who hates you."

"The people were also told to 'do good to them that hate you.' Do you think you could do good things for him as well as mention him in your prayers?" asked Sister Day.

All the girls were looking straight at AJ. Her cheeks flushed a little. "I don't know," said AJ. "That'd be really hard."

"All right, class," said Sister Day, "instead of just AJ doing this, could everyone do good to Brother Gruen and pray for him?"

Some of the girls nodded.

"During this coming week, I challenge each of you to do at least one good thing for Brother Gruen," said Sister Day. "And every morning and every night when you say your prayers, ask Heavenly Father to bless him. All right?"

The class unanimously agreed.

That afternoon, when AJ's family was having Sunday dinner, she looked out the window and into the backyard. She thought of how lonely she was for Miranda.

"AJ," said her father, interrupting her thoughts, "what did you study in your class today at church?"

"First of all we talked about our service project," replied AJ. "Then I told them about Miranda knocking Brother Gruen on the floor and how he had the police take her away. Sister Day said that we should all do good for him and pray for him."

"I don't know if I'd do anything good for him," said Sara. "I think he's a mean man."

"Maybe our family should mention Brother Gruen in our family prayers," said AJ's mother. "And I think it's a good idea to do something nice for him."

"I agree," said Grandma. "Anyone who loves flowers the way he does can't be all bad. Besides, lots of people praying for him and doing good things for him just might bring him around to understanding that loving is better than hating."

That night in their family prayer, Jen asked Heavenly Father to bless Brother Gruen with a good feeling in his heart. Later, as AJ knelt beside her bed, she again asked Heavenly Father to bless him. She felt a little strange inside. She really didn't like him. But she remembered her promise to Sister Day.

Her thoughts turned to the story Sister Day had told them in class. She could envision the Savior sitting on a mountainside and telling stories to the people. Then she thought of another special person who was across the ocean. He was telling some of the same stories to people in Germany. Her heart ached for her big brother, Benj. She wished he were home to help her with her problem. But somehow she knew that his advice would be much the same as what Sister Day had given.

AJ glanced over at Sara's bed. She was already asleep, so AJ's desk lamp wouldn't disturb her. AJ took out some paper and a pen. "Dear Benj," she began. It was late into the night when AJ finally finished her letter to her big brother and shut off the light. She fell asleep wondering what she could do for Brother Gruen.

Foxglove—beauty in solitude, admiration

9

Shopping with Grandma

"What are you going to do for Brother Gruen?" Emily asked as she and AJ walked past his house on their way to school.

"I don't know," said AJ. "But it looks like some-one from our class has already done something." A brightly covered package with a big red bow was sitting on Brother Gruen's porch.

"My mom suggested inviting him to dinner," said Emily. "But I doubt if he'd come."

"I know for sure he wouldn't come to our home," said AJ. "But he might come to yours. It's just that right now he really hates me. I'll have to do something for him that he doesn't even have to see me do."

Emily and AJ ran into the school just before the warning bell rang. "We'd better hurry so we're not late for class," said Emily. "Miss Bleezer's been in a pretty good mood lately, and I don't want to make her mad."

As AJ worked on her math, her mind kept wandering. She thought of Miranda and wondered how she was doing at the pound. She thought of her mean old neighbor. All he had done for her was to cause trouble. How could she be nice to him?

Sister Day's words flashed into her mind—*do good to those who despitefully use you.* If there was something good about him . . . if there was something he did good . . .

"That's it," AJ whispered. "His flowers."

"Do you have a question, AJ?" asked Miss Bleezer.

AJ realized she must have talked louder than she thought. "No," AJ answered. "I was just trying to solve a problem, and I think I've got an answer." She didn't think she should explain that it was not a math problem that had occupied her thoughts.

AJ was so excited. She was glad when the bell rang to go home so she could talk to Emily.

"Em, I think I know what I'll do for Brother Gruen," AJ said enthusiastically. "You know how he must love flowers?"

"Yes," said Emily.

"I'm going to leave him flowers every day on his porch," said AJ. "And I'll leave a poem with them."

"That's a great idea!" exclaimed Emily. "I knew you'd come up with something creative to win him over."

"I don't know about winning him over," said AJ. "But he must love flowers—he has so many of them! I just hope this works."

"When are you going to start?" Emily asked.

"As soon as I get home," AJ answered. "I'll ask Mom or Grandma if they can take me to the store. Do you want to come with us?"

"No, thanks," Emily answered. Her enthusiasm for the idea waned. "You and your grandma go. You two don't need anyone else around."

AJ felt a strange feeling inside as though she'd hurt her best friend's feelings.

"I'll call you tonight and let you know what I find," said AJ.

"You don't have to," said Emily, turning toward her yard.

"Should we put them on his doorstep when we go to school in the morning?" asked AJ.

"That'd be fun," said Emily. "But if you and your grandma decide to do it, that's okay."

AJ watched as Emily walked up to her doorstep. *What's bothering her?* AJ wondered. *Why is she acting like this?*

AJ turned toward her house. As she entered the back door, she spotted her mother at the kitchen counter. "Hi, Mom. Is there any chance you can get away to take me to the store? I think I know what I can do for Brother Gruen."

"Sure," her mother replied, "if you can wait for about an hour. I've got someone coming to check the fridge. It's been acting kind of funny today."

"If you need to go right now, I can take you," said Grandma coming into the kitchen.

"Can you really?" asked AJ. "I don't have any homework, and I'd sure like to go now if it's okay."

"That'd be fine," said AJ's mother, "as long as Grandma doesn't mind driving the Suburban."

"I think I can drive that big old thing," said Grandma. "That is, if you trust me with it."

AJ's mother laughed. "I trust you with anything," she said.

"Give me a minute to get my money," said AJ. She rushed into her room and took out her bank. She had been saving for a long time, and her bank was getting full. She took two five-dollar bills with her. *I hope this is enough,* she thought.

When she and Grandma were in the car, Grandma asked her, "Now where is it we're going?"

"I don't know for sure," said AJ. "Where do you think they'd have flowers?"

"I think I saw a nursery not far from here," suggested Grandma. "Did you say these are for Brother Gruen?"

"They sure are," said AJ. "Remember that you told me that someone who likes flowers like he does can't be all bad? I plan to leave him flowers on his doorstep every morning this week."

"That's a marvelous idea!" said Grandma. "Are you going to tell him who they're from?"

"At first, I thought I'd leave them anonymously," said AJ. "But the more I thought about, I think he needs to know I'm the one leaving them. I want him to know that I'm willing to be friends with him."

"I'm proud of you, AJ," said Grandma. "Most kids your age would be so mad at him they'd never do anything nice for him. Here you are trying to be his friend."

"I was mad at him, Grandma," said AJ. "At first I didn't want to ever see him again. But the more I've thought about him, the more I feel sorry for him. I don't think he's got anyone who cares about him."

"You're quite the character," said Grandma as she

drove into the nursery's parking lot. "Here we are. Let's find us some flowers."

"May I help you?" asked the nurseryman.

"I need some flowers," said AJ. "They're for someone who loves flowers and has a yard filled with them."

"Do you want annuals or perennials?" he asked.

AJ looked confused. "I don't know. I need something that's pretty."

"We'd probably like flowers that he can plant in his yard," said Grandma. "Since perennials come up every year, could you show us some of those?"

"Over here I have some beautiful daisies that are almost in full bloom," said the nurseryman. "These bright yellow ones are my favorite."

AJ's eyes lit with excitement. "Those are beautiful!" she exclaimed. "How much are they?"

"This particular plant is $5.98, but I do have some less expensive ones," he said.

"I've got only ten dollars," said AJ. "I need to buy six plants."

"Hm-m-m." The nurseryman looked around at his plants. "I think I've got just the thing for you," he said. "Do you like violets? I have several of these."

AJ liked the deep purple ones.

He led her over to more plants. "And here are some snapdragons, asters, and lilies."

AJ looked puzzled. Turning to her grandmother, she said, "I don't know, Grandma. Which ones should I buy?"

Grandma smiled. "You probably didn't think you'd have such a big selection of plants. Why don't you just buy the daisies today. You can think about the others, and we'll come back tomorrow."

AJ agreed. Buying six different plants was too big a decision. And she knew she didn't have enough money with her. She turned to the nurseryman.

"Thank you for showing me all your flowers," she said. "Could I take the daisies today and then come back tomorrow for some others?"

"Of course," he said. "I'll still have plenty tomorrow. Are these to be a gift?"

"Yes," answered AJ. "They're for my neighbor."

"In that case, how about some gold foil around the pot and a big yellow bow to match?" asked the nurseryman. He noticed AJ fumbling with her money. "No cost," he added.

"Sure," said AJ. "That'd be great!"

AJ held the plant carefully as Grandmother drove toward home. "Grandma, how about an ice cream cone? I still have some money, and I'd love to buy you a treat."

"Sounds wonderful," said Grandma. "But let me buy it."

"No way," said AJ. "You were so good to take me to buy flowers, and now it's my turn to treat you."

Grandmother pulled into the drive-in window and ordered two soft chocolate ice cream cones. AJ slipped some coins into Grandma's hand.

As Grandma drove toward home, she and AJ talked about giving the flowers to their neighbor. "Now I need to write a poem to go with them," said AJ.

Suddenly and without warning, a large shaggy dog jumped in front of the Suburban. AJ screamed as Grandmother swerved sharply to miss it. The daisies fell to the floor in a heap.

10

Flowers and Poems

"Are you all right?" Grandmother asked breathlessly as she pulled over to the side of the road.

"Sure, I'm fine," answered AJ. "But look at the daisies."

The yellow flowers were covered with dirt.

"I think they're ruined," said AJ.

Grandma stopped the car and got out. She walked over to AJ's side and opened the door. "They're just a little messed," she said, observing the tipped pot. "I'm just glad you're all right. I shouldn't have swerved so sharply."

"But you missed the dog," said AJ.

Grandma quickly picked up the yellow flowers, scooped the soil back inside the pot, and shook the yellow ribbon free of dirt. "There," she said, handing the pot to AJ, "hold on to this for dear life in case another dog runs across the street."

Their eyes met. Both broke into laughter.

"Oh, Grandma, you can make even terrible moments turn into good ones," said AJ. "I wish I were more like you. I thought the flowers were ruined."

Grandma chuckled as she started the car. "You have to remember, AJ, I've had a lot more practice. When I was your age, I would've thought the flowers were ruined too. But through the years, I've learned that many a tipped plant just needs the dirt stuffed back inside and the dirt brushed off the petals."

"As soon as we get home, I'm going to write a poem to go with this," said AJ. "In the morning, Emily and I are going to leave it on Brother Gruen's porch when we go to school."

"I know he'll love both the flowers and the poem," said Grandmother.

When they reached home, AJ took the plant and put it in the middle of her desk. She started to write:

> Roses are red,
> Violets are blue,
> I hope you enjoy
> These flowers for you.

She sat and studied the poem. *That's really dumb,* she thought. *I need to write him a real poem. One that really means something to him.* She began again:

> I love to see your flowers
> As I pass your home each day.
> They brighten up our neighborhood;
> They almost seem to say:
> "We hope this day is happy,

We wish you all that's good,
We're glad to be a part
Of this neighborhood."
Thanks, Brother Gruen, for making our
neighborhood such a beautiful place to live.
Your Friend,
AJ

AJ rewrote the poem and note on bright yellow stationery to match the bow on the daisies and tucked it in the flowers. She could hardly wait for tomorrow morning.

Daisy—innocence, pure in thought, loyal in love and beauty

That night, AJ kept thinking about what other flowers to buy. She didn't want to spend too much money. She was also hoping that someday she could send Miranda to obedience school, and she knew that would not be cheap.

Miranda. How she missed Miranda! It was still a whole week before she'd be able to come home.

Early next morning, AJ spotted Emily waiting for her on the corner. "Hi, Em," AJ called.

Emily hesitated until she spotted the yellow daisies. Then she ran over to AJ.

"I love your flowers," Emily said. "Are we going to ring the doorbell, leave them on his front porch, and run?"

"It's kind of early," said AJ. "If he's not up, the doorbell might bother him. Let's leave them on the porch and hope he sees them. Okay?"

The girls ran up to Brother Gruen's porch and placed the bright yellow daisies right in front of his door.

"He'll be surprised when he sees these," said Emily. "What did you write in your poem?"

AJ told Emily what her poem said. "I hope he doesn't think it's dumb," she said.

"Don't worry," said Emily. "With beautiful flowers and a poem, he's bound to crack a smile."

The girls left for school. All day, AJ's thoughts wandered back and forth to the flowers, Brother Gruen, and Miranda. But as she and Emily walked home from school, her heart sank.

"Oh, Em," AJ moaned. "The flowers are still on his porch. He must not have wanted them."

"Be sensible, AJ," said Emily. "He's probably not had a reason to open his front door. Maybe he'll find them when his paper's delivered later this afternoon. By the way, do you want to come over to my house for a while? We can get something to eat."

"Can't," said AJ. "Grandma and I have to go to the florist again for some more flowers."

Emily shrugged her shoulders and turned toward her yard without saying good-bye.

"Thanks for asking," said AJ. "Maybe I can come over tomorrow."

Emily kept walking away without a word.

I wonder what's bothering her, AJ thought. But she had too much on her mind to worry about Emily right now.

As soon as AJ entered her front door, Grandma was there with a grin. "Look what I've found, AJ," she said enthusiastically. "Here's all kinds of information on flowers."

She showed AJ her book, and together they browsed through the pages looking at the many kinds of flowers that grew well in Utah.

"Maybe buying him flowers isn't such a good idea," said AJ. "Emily and I left the daisies on his front porch, and they're still sitting there."

"Don't get discouraged," said Grandma. "Why don't you grab a snack and then we'll go to the florist."

AJ couldn't resist Grandma's enthusiasm. She grabbed a handful of peanuts from off the counter, then ran to take more money from her bank.

"I hope these don't cost too much," she called downstairs to Grandma.

As Grandma drove toward the florist shop, AJ read the book on flowers.

"Grandma, it says here that flowers have their own language. They stand for different things. Daisies are for innocence."

AJ started laughing. "And listen to this. Tulips are a declaration of love. It was mostly his tulips that Miranda ruined. But for sure, I'm not giving Brother Gruen tulips."

"What about zinnias?" asked Grandmother. "And

73

marigolds, lilies, violets, and geraniums. Do they all mean different things too?"

"They do!" exclaimed AJ. "Zinnias stand for thoughts of absent friends. That'd be a good one for Brother Gruen. And here's something on violets. They stand for loyalty and faithfulness. I don't know how I could work those in."

"I figure you need five more plants if you're delivering the last one on Sunday. Is that right?" Grandmother asked.

"Right," said AJ. "Maybe we should get the plants first and then worry about the poems and what they stand for. But for sure, I'm not getting him any tulips!"

Grandma laughed.

"I see you came back," said the florist as Grandma and AJ entered the store. "Have you decided which ones you want?"

"I need five more pots of flowers," said AJ. "The most I can spend is ten dollars. Do you think I can get five plants for that much?"

"Sure," said the florist. "Over here I have some wonderful geranium plants. They aren't in full bloom yet, but they are still pretty and will blossom throughout the summer. Here are some pansies. They're inexpensive and yet very pretty. Of course, I've got some beautiful rose bushes. They cost a little more, but the small ones aren't too much. What do you think?"

AJ looked confused. "What do you think, Grandma?" she asked.

"Hmmm," mused Grandma. "You tell me which ones you think your neighbor would like."

"How about the geranium, some pansies, one of

the small red rose bushes, and some of the zinnias," said AJ walking around the different kinds of flowers. "And how about a lily for Sunday morning? How much would that cost?"

The florist smiled. "You've made some good choices. Since these are for gifts, you can have my special customer discount, which brings the total to $8.98."

AJ took out her wallet. "Does that include wrapping?" she asked.

"That includes wrapping and a bow to match," replied the florist.

AJ was ecstatic as she carried the beautiful flowers to the car.

"I sure hope we don't encounter any dogs this afternoon," said Grandma, securing her seat belt.

As they neared their neighborhood, AJ exclaimed, "Grandma! Brother Gruen has taken the daisies off his porch!"

Sure enough. The porch was empty, just waiting for some more flowers.

That evening, AJ sat by her desk with all of the plants surrounding her.

First I'll write a poem about the geranium, AJ thought. She consulted Grandma's book. Geraniums mean "comfort." But what could she write about comfort? She thought for a minute and then wrote:

If ever you have a horrible day
And you wish for it to end,
Look at this red geranium
And remember you have a friend—
ME!
AJ

AJ hurried and copied it on red paper to match the flower. Next she looked at the little purple pansies. The book said that pansies mean "thinking of you."

That would be an easy poem to write, she thought.

THURSDAY BLAHS
Sometimes Thursday is not too exciting,
It's just a plain, old ordinary day,
But on this special Thursday, be happy,
These pansies have a message. They say—
I'M THINKING OF YOU!
Your Friend,
AJ

Pansy—remembrance, thinking of you

Wow! Two poems ready to use. She looked at the miniature rosebush. According to the book, a red rose means "love", a white rose means "I am worthy of you," and a yellow rose means "jealousy." *I'm glad I didn't choose a yellow rosebush,* she thought.

AJ pulled back the tiny, immature petals to make sure the flower was really red.

If a red rose means love, then a red rosebush with lots of red roses must mean lots of love, thought AJ.

RED ROSE BUSHES
If one single red rose means love,
And this bush has many a red bloom,
Just imagine how very much love
This bush brings to your living room.
Your Friend,
AJ

Rose—love

"AJ!" her father called. "It's time for family prayer. Can you leave your lessons just a minute to come down into the family room?"

AJ looked at her clock. She couldn't believe it was getting so late. And she still had loads of homework. She ran down the stairs to join her family.

"I was writing poems to go with the flowers for Brother Gruen," she said. "I still have two to write, but I don't know if I can get them done, with all my homework."

"You can finish them tomorrow," said her mother. "You'd better get to bed."

It was Sara's turn to say the prayer. After she asked blessings upon everyone in the family, she asked Heavenly Father to bless Brother Gruen that he would like the flowers. "And bless AJ that she can think of two more poems," she added.

After the prayer, AJ grinned at her little sister. "Thanks, Sara," she said. "You hurry and get ready for bed, and I promise not to keep the light on very long, okay?"

"Are you going to let me read the poems?" Grandma asked as they walked upstairs.

"Of course," said AJ. "Let me hurry and finish two more, and I'll bring them to your room."

AJ turned the flower book to zinnias—"thoughts of absent friends." This would be a hard one.

FRIENDS FOREVER
Friends come into our lives
When we're young and when we're old.
Be grateful for your treasured friends
They're worth much more than gold.

I'm glad you're my friend,
AJ

Maybe if I keep signing the word friend, *he'll get the message,* mused AJ.

"And now the lily," AJ said quietly. "This is the last one!"

"Which one is the lily?" asked Sara, peeking out from under the covers on her bed.

"It's this beautiful white flower," said AJ holding it up for Sara to see. "This flower stands for purity. It blooms in the spring at Easter time."

"Hurry and write your poem, okay?" said Sara. "I'm getting tired."

"I'll hurry," promised AJ.

Sara's prayer must have helped, because in no time at all AJ had the last poem written.

She quietly turned out the light even though Sara was sound asleep. Then she tiptoed towards Grandma's room, in case she was asleep too.

"I'm so glad you're still awake," said AJ, noticing Grandma reading in bed. "Do you still want to hear my poems?"

"Of course."

She read each one without saying a word. After reading AJ's note to Brother Gruen at the end of her last poem, tears filled Grandma's eyes. "You're really something," she said warmly. "I wish I could write like you do."

AJ hugged Grandmother, wished her a goodnight, and slipped into her own room. She still had homework, so she turned the light back on and did it quickly and quietly. Even though she was tired, AJ could hardly wait for morning, when she and Emily would leave the geranium on Brother Gruen's porch.

Poppy (red)—comfort

11

The Final Delivery

"Hi, AJ," Emily called as she waited on the corner. "Looks like you have another flower for Brother Gruen."

"Grandma found a book that explained what different flowers mean," said AJ. "She took me to the florist, and now I've got all the flowers for the rest of the week. I've written a poem about each one."

Emily's blue eyes met AJ's brown ones. "Does your grandma do everything for you?" Emily asked sarcastically.

AJ's heart quickened. "Why did you ask that?" AJ replied defensively. "She's been helping me with this project. And I've appreciated your being so excited about this idea, too. Are you mad at me for giving these flowers to Brother Gruen?"

Emily's cheeks flushed. "It's not the flowers. It's . . . uh . . ."

"It's what?" asked AJ. "Why don't you tell me what's wrong?"

Emily's eyes betrayed her hurt feelings. "It's just that ever since your grandmother came, you never want to do anything with me. It's always Grandma this and Grandma that."

AJ stood quietly, holding the flowers. "I'm sorry," she finally said. "I thought you liked my grandma."

"Oh, it's not your grandma," said Emily. "I do like her. It's just that you don't care about anyone except her anymore."

"That's not true, Em. You're my best friend."

"Not anymore," said Emily. She turned and started in the direction of the school.

AJ watched Emily walk away. She placed the geranium on Brother Gruen's porch and followed Emily. But Emily kept walking.

The rest of the week dragged. Without Emily, leaving the flowers wasn't nearly as much fun. AJ also missed walking home with her.

Early Saturday morning, AJ was dressed and ready to deliver the zinnias. *I wish Emily was meeting me on the corner,* she thought. *I miss her coming with me to deliver the flowers.*

She straightened the card and was off to Brother Gruen's. She placed the zinnias where the other plants had been. Tomorrow she would deliver the last flower. She might never know how he felt about them, but at least the project was nearly over.

AJ raced home, arriving just in time to join her family for breakfast.

"Did you deliver your flowers already?" her mother asked.

"Yes," answered AJ. "I wish I knew if Brother Gruen was liking them or not."

"Some of my friends saw you leaving flowers on his doorstep this week and asked me what you were doing," said Jen. "I told them about your project, and they think it's a terrific idea!"

"You have to feel good knowing that you're doing your part," said her father. "Besides, it won't be long before Miranda comes home; maybe the flowers will soften Brother Gruen's hard heart towards her."

"You know how Miranda doesn't obey me very well?" AJ said to her father. "I've been thinking about taking her to obedience school. I hope I've got enough money saved to pay for it."

Grandma's eyes lighted. "I think that's a brilliant idea! Miranda's smart and would catch on quickly. If you decide to take her, I'll pay for at least half of her lessons. Okay?"

"Grandma, you don't have to pay anything," said AJ. "But I could use some help taking her to class. The only school I could find around here is way out on the other side of town."

"Consider me your taxi," said Grandma. "Before long I'll be known as the Grandma in the BMW."

Everyone looked confused. "BMW?" Jen asked.

"Of course," laughed Grandma. "In St. George, all the grandparents call the Suburbans 'Big Mormon Wagons.'"

"I like that," said Jake. "From now on, I'll tell my friends that my grandma drives a BMW." The family laughed.

"Saturday chore time," Mother reminded everyone.

A few groans escaped, but the family knew what had to be done. Soon the vacuum was running, a load of clothes was thrown in the washer, and the regular Saturday work was in process.

Luckily we have a big family, thought AJ. With everyone helping, the house got cleaned pretty fast.

"Mom, I finished cleaning the bathrooms and vacuuming the basement," AJ called to her mother. "Is it all right if I go outside and work on Miranda's doghouse?"

"Make sure your room is all picked up," Mom replied.

Sara sure is messy, AJ thought as she picked up Sara's stuffed animals and dancing outfit. *She leaves everything out.*

Sara was busy vacuuming the stairs, so AJ decided to clean their room by herself. At times like this, she missed having her own room.

"I'm all done," she called to her mother. "I'll be outside with Dad."

AJ walked around their house to the back yard. "You sure did a good job with Miranda's dog run," AJ said to her father as he trimmed some bushes. "Do we have much more to do on the doghouse?"

"It's almost done," he replied. "We only need to paint it."

"Would you trust me to paint it?" she asked. "I'd be really careful."

"That's a great idea!" said her father. "Let me help you get the paint, and the job is yours."

All afternoon, AJ was busy painting Miranda's doghouse. When the second coat was nearly dry, AJ decided that Miranda's name should be on the front. She scouted around for blue paint. AJ was pleased to see how good it looked as she carefully brushed on each letter. She could hardly wait for Miranda to come home.

Early next morning, AJ was up and showering.

"Why are you up so early?" asked Grandma. "Usually on Sundays, you like to sleep in a little."

"Not today," said AJ. "I need to deliver Brother Gruen's last flower today. I think I'll do it first thing this morning."

She sat on the edge of Grandma's bed and brushed her long brown hair.

"Is Emily meeting you?" Grandma asked.

AJ quit brushing her hair. "She's mad at me," said AJ.

"Anything you'd care to share?" Grandma asked.

"She's mad at me for spending so much time with you," AJ blurted. "I think it's childish."

Grandma sat beside AJ. "Remember when you told me that Emily said she and her grandmother didn't spend much time together?"

AJ nodded.

"She probably can't relate to our relationship. But I can't have you two break up a good friendship because of me."

AJ flashed a grin at her grandmother. "It's not your fault, Grandma. I guess I've been a little rude to Em. I was so excited when you and I went to the florist that I forgot about her. I should have invited her to come with us. I think I can understand how she feels."

"Where's the hair spray?" Jen shouted from the bathroom. "Does anyone know?"

Grandma's eyes widened. She hurried to the bathroom and opened the side cabinet.

"Here it is, Jen," she said apologetically. "I didn't know where it belonged so I put it in here. Sorry."

Jen acted disgusted as Grandma handed her the hair spray.

AJ sensed the hurt Grandma felt. She faced her big sister and exclaimed, "This bathroom is for all of us! Don't act like it's only yours!"

Jen glared at AJ. "All I ask is that next time the hair spray is where it belongs," she said, stamping out of the room.

"C'mon, Grandma," said AJ. "Jen's in a horrible mood this morning. Why don't you come and deliver this lily with me?"

"You go ahead, AJ," said Grandma. "I don't feel up to it right now."

The door to Grandma's room widened, revealing Jen in the doorway with a sheepish look on her face. "Sorry, Grandma," she said. "I shouldn't have been so rude to you." She walked over and put her arms around her grandmother.

Grandma's eyes filled with tears.

"AJ," said Jen, "while you deliver your lily, Grandma and I are going to have a talk on how granddaughters, especially teenage granddaughters, should treat their grandmothers."

It's about time, thought AJ. As she left Grandma's room, she overheard Jen apologize for being selfish and unkind. AJ smiled. This would make Grandma feel a lot better.

"Bye," AJ called to Grandma and Jen. "Wish me luck. I hope Brother Gruen doesn't yell at me."

"Good luck," Grandma and Jen echoed.

AJ's mother was in the kitchen. " 'Bye, Mom. I'm going to deliver this lily to Brother Gruen. This morning I think I'll ring his doorbell and give him the flowers in person. Do you think that's a good idea?"

Her mother smiled. "I like that idea," she said. "Besides, I think you'll be able to find out how much he's enjoyed the other flowers. If you get a chance, you can even invite him to go to church."

"Wouldn't that shock everyone if he came?" exclaimed AJ. "I can imagine the looks on everyone's face if he walked in and sat down."

AJ picked up the white lily and card. "Wish me luck," she said.

"Good luck," said her mother. "I have a feeling all will turn out just great!"

AJ left her home with a nervous feeling in her stomach. *I hope he's not asleep,* she worried. *Maybe I should just leave this on his front porch after all.*

But the closer she got to Brother Gruen's home, the more determined she was to give the lily to him in person. She took a deep breath and rang the doorbell. Her heart raced. What if he yelled at her?

She stood waiting. She peeked through the glass panel by his door. She thought she could see him standing in his kitchen. She looked closer. She was about to ring the doorbell again, when she stopped abruptly. Smoke—she could smell smoke!

Again, she looked through the glass panel. "Oh, no!" gasped AJ. Not only could she smell smoke but could also see it in Brother Gruen's kitchen. Quickly AJ grabbed the door knob, but the door was locked. She rang the bell again, but Brother Gruen paid no attention.

"He's in trouble!" exclaimed AJ. She rushed to his back door by the kitchen. She threw open the door and was horrified at the sight!

12

AJ to the Rescue

AJ quickly laid the lily on the kitchen table and ran to Brother Gruen's side. Flames were leaping from the stove to his side counter.

"Grab the towel!" shouted AJ. "Get the towel wet and smother the flames!"

Brother Gruen staggered around the table as if he didn't know what was going on.

"Where's your soda?" yelled AJ. "We need baking soda to throw on the fire."

Brother Gruen pointed toward a side cupboard as he reached for the towel. To AJ's horror, instead of getting the towel wet and smothering the flames, he threw the towel at the fire. The flames grabbed hold of the dry fabric.

AJ spied the box of soda and threw soda on the flames coming from the pan on the stove. She managed to remove the burning pan and throw it into the sink. Flames were still leaping at the side cupboard, trying to reach the curtains. AJ tore the curtains from the rods, doused them in water and smothered the flames.

"I've got it!" she yelled in relief. AJ turned to find Brother Gruen—and shouted in horror, "Fall on the floor! Fall on the floor!"

Brother Gruen's shirt sleeve was on fire, and he was too dazed to know what to do. AJ grabbed the wet curtains and jumped toward him, knocking him to the floor. She buried his sleeve in the curtains and kept pounding the damp material into the flame.

"Stop hitting me!" yelled the old man. "Stop hitting me! You're hurting me!"

AJ paid no attention to him. She had to get the fire out, and she continued to pound on the wet curtains to douse the flame on his shirt.

Brother Gruen was infuriated. "Stop hitting me!" he yelled again.

When AJ tried to stand, the torn curtain snagged her foot and she tumbled into the table. She winced in pain as the table leg jabbed her side. Fearfully, she glanced around to make sure the fire was out. To her relief, all the flames were extinguished. She watched the old man stagger to stand up.

Grabbing hold of her throbbing side, she pulled herself up by the table.

"Why were you hitting me?" yelled the old man.

AJ couldn't believe his words. Instead of yelling back at him, she was so relieved that the fire was out that she collapsed in a chair. Calmly she replied, "I wasn't hitting you to hurt you. I was trying to put out the fire that was burning your shirt sleeve."

Brother Gruen didn't say a word. He stood looking at AJ as though he were trying to figure out exactly what had happened.

"I came to give you a flower," said AJ, "and I found you back here in your kitchen. I guess when you were fixing your breakfast, the grease in your pan caught on fire. That's why I grabbed your soda and threw it on the flames."

"You weren't hitting me?" he asked bewildered.

"No, I'd never do anything to hurt you," said AJ. "I guess that's why you and I don't understand each other very well. Every time I come to visit you, I come to be your friend. But you always think I'm here to hurt you or do something bad to you. Remember when my dog jumped on you?"

Brother Gruen nodded.

"She only wanted the cinnamon rolls. She didn't want to hurt you. And today, when I tried to help you, you thought I was hurting you. We just don't understand each other very well."

Smoke filtered through the dreary kitchen. AJ opened the back door and windows to let the smoke out.

"I'm sorry," said Brother Gruen. He feebly took hold of a chair and sat down. "By the way, are you all right?" he asked, noticing AJ holding her side.

To AJ's amazement, Brother Gruen seemed sincerely concerned about her.

"Sure, I'm okay," she answered. "How's your arm? Did the fire burn through your shirt?"

She walked over and together they examined the tattered sleeve.

"I'm fine," he said. "My shirt's just burned, and

the hair on my arm is singed, but that's all—thanks to you!"

"If you're okay, I'd better be going home," said AJ.

"C-could you stay for a few more minutes?" Brother Gruen asked. "I'd feel better if you didn't leave quite yet."

AJ was surprised. Instead of an ornery old man who yelled at her, she saw instead a tired and lonely person who was a bit frightened and didn't want to be alone. Grandma's words echoed in her mind. "Look at him as though he were young—with hair— no wrinkles. Discover what he's like inside."

"Why don't you sit here for a little while, and I'll clean up your kitchen," said AJ. "You can talk to me. Okay?"

Brother Gruen nodded. He spotted the lily on the kitchen table.

"So you brought me another flower," he said. "Why have you been bringing me flowers every day?"

AJ smiled as she gathered the ripped curtains. She was glad he had noticed the lily.

"I think I've ruined your curtains," she said. "I'll buy you some new ones."

"Forget the curtains," said Brother Gruen. "Tell me, why have you been bringing me flowers?"

"I didn't know any other way to do something nice for you," said AJ. "But I know you like flowers, because you have such a beautiful yard filled with them."

"Why did you want to do something nice for me?" he asked. "I've never gone out of my way to be friendly to you."

AJ stood at the sink washing dishes. "Remember

the day my Merrie Miss class came to visit?" she asked.

"Yes," he said, "and I met your grandmother."

"That's right," said AJ. "We came to visit to try and make you feel comfortable so you'd come out to church. Then when my dog jumped on you and you had the police take her away, I knew you'd never be happy to see me."

AJ started laughing.

"I don't understand what's so funny," said Brother Gruen. He was somewhat perplexed.

"I was thinking about what Grandma said about you," said AJ.

"Tell me what she said," grunted Brother Gruen. "Did she tell you to forget about such a grumpy old man?"

"Quite the opposite," said AJ. "She said you are like an old sock who's filled with holes."

"An old sock?" he asked unbelievingly.

"An old sock! She said that old socks still have lots of wear in them if we take the time to mend the holes. Grandma said I should mend some of your holes so you wouldn't be so ornery."

Brother Gruen grunted. "So you've been mending my holes with these flowers?"

AJ turned to look at him. "Have they done any good?" she asked.

Brother Gruen relaxed and a faint smile crossed his face. "The first day you brought me daisies, I thought you were trying to bribe me into telling the police to forget about keeping your dog. But when a new flower appeared on my porch every morning, I knew you weren't playing tricks."

"And did they make you feel good?" AJ asked, putting the last of the dishes away.

"They made me realize that I've been a stubborn old man," he said. "By the way, I surely did like those poems you wrote. My little girl . . ." His voice trailed off.

AJ walked over to his side. "What did you say about your little girl?" she asked.

"Never mind," said Brother Gruen. "That really isn't important."

"Yes, it is," said AJ. "Please tell me what you were going to say about your little girl."

Brother Gruen's eyes filled with tears. "My little girl used to write poems for me. But that was many, many years ago."

"What happened?" AJ asked.

"Let's talk about your flowers," he said, trying to change the subject.

"I'd rather hear about your daughter," said AJ persistently. She drew up a chair and sat close to the old man so she could hear every word.

"It was so long ago," he began. "But I can still hear her giggling, and I still can see her coming through the front door and shouting, 'Hi, Dad. I'm home.'"

"What happened to her?" asked AJ.

"My wife and I decided to take her to visit her grandparents. It was in the spring. A terrible hailstorm hit, and I couldn't see the cars in front of us. A truck jackknifed ahead of us, and I couldn't see it until it was too late. We hit the truck pretty hard. We were all taken to the hospital, and I had a severe concussion. When I finally came to, it was weeks later. I was told that my wife and daughter had been buried."

AJ sat quietly, not knowing what to say.

"When I moved into your neighborhood, the first time I caught a glimpse of you, it was like seeing my daughter again. I watched you jump the rope and ride your bike. I saw you playing catch with your dad, and you both acted so happy. I grew angry. Why should you and your family be so happy when I was so miserable? But now I realize that I wasn't angry at you. All this time, I've been angry at myself. I've not been able to forgive myself for driving into that truck."

"But you must have had some good feelings," said AJ. "Grandma said that people who raise beautiful flowers can't be all bad."

"I've got to get to know your grandmother," said Brother Gruen. "She sounds like a pretty wise person."

"She really is," agreed AJ. "And you'd like her. She's a lot of fun. But tell me, why did you keep growing flowers when you felt so bad inside?"

Brother Gruen thought for a minute. "I guess my love for flowers began when I was released from the hospital. It was in late spring when the flowers were all blooming. I took a bunch to the graves of my wife and my daughter. For some reason, I kept planting flowers so I'd always have plenty for their graves."

"Do you still visit their graves?" asked AJ.

"At least once a week I walk to the cemetery. It's not too far from here," he said.

"Could I go with you next week?" asked AJ. "I'd love to visit their graves with you."

"You're quite the girl, AJ Bexton," said Brother Gruen. "I've been so terrible to you. I can't believe you'd give me another chance."

"Actually, it was my fault you got mad at me," said AJ. "When my dog tore up your flower bed, you had a reason to get mad."

"I was pretty angry," he agreed. "But after I called the police and had your dog taken away, I felt like a fool. I knew she was after the rolls when she knocked me down. I was too darn stubborn to admit it."

"Well, I'm saving my money, and I'm going to send her to obedience school," said AJ. "Grandma says Miranda's really smart and will learn to obey what I say. I don't think you'll have to worry about her getting in your garden again."

Brother Gruen glanced at the lily on the table. "That's a pretty lily you brought," he said.

"This is my Sunday flower to you," said AJ. She handed the flower and card to Brother Gruen.

Silently, he read the poem.

THE LILY
The lily stands for purity;
The white petals seem to say,
Do what is right, do what is kind,
Heaven's blessings will come your way.

Lily—purity, sweetness, sincerity

Then he read the note.

Dear Brother Gruen,

    This week I have left flowers at your doorstep. I read in a book that flowers have a language, and each flower gives a message just by being itself. It seems that every time I have come to speak with you, we have ended up in a fight. I hope these flowers have told you the things that I wanted to say but couldn't. Maybe you don't want to be my friend, but I'm going to be yours.

                   Your Friend,
                      AJ

After a long silence, Brother Gruen looked at AJ.

"Thanks, AJ. You've taught an old man a lesson he should have learned a long time ago. If my daughter had lived, perhaps I'd have had a granddaughter much like you."

"Guess I'd better go home," said AJ. "I still have to get ready for church." She stopped at the kitchen door.

"Brother Gruen, would you like to go to church with me today?" she asked.

"Oh, no, I can't do that," he said. "You've got your family to go with and—"

"And we'd love it if you'd come with us," interjected AJ. She walked over to her new friend. "Why don't you get all ready, and we'll stop by for you at a quarter to twelve. Okay?"

"Are you sure?" he asked.

"I'm sure!" said AJ.

13

A Beautiful Language

AJ raced home. She felt so good inside. *Wow! It really does help to pray for your enemies,* she thought as she entered her front door.

"AJ!" exclaimed Grandma, "What has happened to you?"

AJ glanced in the hall mirror and started laughing. Black soot was on her face and clothes. She smelled like smoke. "I've been in a fire," she said.

"Are you all right?" Grandma asked, concerned.

"I've never felt better," said AJ. "Oh, Grandma, you truly are a wise person, just like Brother Gruen said."

Grandma was baffled. "Brother Gruen said I was wise?"

"I've got so much to tell you," said AJ. "In fact, I think the whole family needs to hear this."

Grandma called everyone to come into her room. After hearing about the fire and making sure AJ was unharmed, her family sat around her as she told about Brother Gruen and his wife and daughter.

"When he asked why I left the flowers, I told him that Grandma said he was like an old sock that needed mending. He laughed when I told him that the flowers were part of my mending project."

"And do you like him now?" asked Sara, her big brown eyes full of wonderment.

"I sure do," said AJ. "And you won't believe what I'm going to tell you. Brother Gruen is going to church with us today."

"Hooray!" shouted Sara. "Can I sit by him in sacrament meeting. Please?"

"For sure, Sara, you can sit by him," said AJ. "I think he'll enjoy getting to know you. If anyone can make him feel lots of love, you're the one!"

Sara beamed.

"We'd better get ready," said AJ's mother. "This is going to be one great Sunday. By the way, did you invite him to Sunday dinner, too?"

"I didn't, Mom," said AJ. "But I have a feeling that it'll be easy to convince him to come."

After everyone left Grandma's room, AJ stopped at the door and grinned at Grandma. "You sure know a lot about old socks."

Grandma smiled. "But you were the one who did the mending."

As the Bextons climbed into their "BMW," AJ couldn't remember another Sunday when they were all so excited to go. As her father pulled up to Brother Gruen's home, AJ held her breath as the door opened. Brother Gruen was all dressed up in a dark suit, white shirt, and a flowered tie.

"Doesn't he look nice?" said Mother.

AJ's Merrie Miss class clambered around AJ wanting to know how she got Brother Gruen to come to church with her family. She promised to tell them when they had class. AJ spotted Emily in the hall. She hurried to her side.

"Em," said AJ. "I'm sorry for being a rotten friend. I missed you when I was delivering Brother Gruen's flowers. And I've felt awful all week."

"You don't need to apologize," said Emily. "Ever since your grandma came, it seemed like you didn't want to be friends anymore. I was in the way."

"No, you weren't," said AJ. "This whole thing has been my fault. I still want us to be friends. Best friends."

Emily grinned. "Are you sure?"

"Positive," said AJ.

The two friends walked down the hall to their Merrie Miss class. When Sister Day entered the room, the girls shared what they had done during the week for Brother Gruen.

"AJ brought him to church today," said one of the girls.

"You melted his heart," said Sister Day. "I'm proud of you girls for going out of your way to show love to someone you didn't even like."

"You gave us the idea," AJ said to her teacher. "In class last week when you told us to pray for Brother Gruen, I didn't know if I could. But the more I prayed for him, the better I felt inside."

"It's kind of wonderful how doing good for someone else always seems to come back to you in even a larger package," said Sister Day. "But how did you get Brother Gruen to come to church with you?"

AJ related the events of the Sunday morning fire.

"I hope everyone keeps doing nice things for him," said AJ. "I know he gets lonely."

The girls promised they'd keep in touch with Brother Gruen.

"And remember to say hello to him this afternoon," reminded Sister Day.

The girls responded to her suggestion. With AJ's family and her Merrie Miss class crowding around him, Brother Gruen enjoyed his Sunday meeting immensely.

It didn't take much coaxing to get Brother Gruen to come to their home for Sunday dinner. Later that afternoon, after a delicious meal, Brother Gruen said he'd better be on his way home.

"Thanks for taking me to church with you," he said. "And thanks for this wonderful meal. I've not eaten anything like this in a long time."

AJ's mother smiled. "We're so glad you came. We hope you'll come again, very soon."

Sara ran up to his side. "My mom bakes really good cookies. Would you like me to bring you some of them?" she asked, her brown eyes shining.

Brother Gruen laughed. "Please do, Sara," he said. "And sometime, why don't you just come and play with me."

"Thanks, AJ," he said with emotion in his voice. "Thanks for *all* you did for me."

Grandmother and AJ stood at the front door watching Brother Gruen walk up the street.

"I can't believe all of this has happened," said AJ. "I must write Benj and tell him all about Brother Gruen. He'll never believe it."

"It'll be a great story for him to share on his mission," said Grandma.

—

"Just think," said AJ, "in two more days, Miranda will be coming home. I can hardly wait."

"It will be good to see her," said Grandma. "By the way, I saw you talking with Emily at church."

"I told her I was sorry," said AJ. "I think everything's all right now."

"I'm going to help your mother with the dishes," said Grandma. "Why don't you run over to Emily's and invite her to come over Monday after school. Maybe we could make cookies or something?"

"Okay, Grandma," said AJ. "I think she'd like that. I'll be back in a little while."

Grandma watched AJ walk up the street to Emily's home. "We'll have a good time baking cookies," she said to herself.

AJ could hardly sleep Monday night.

She was up early Tuesday morning getting ready for school. "AJ," she heard her little sister call. "There's something on the porch."

AJ ran downstairs and opened the front door. On her porch was a beautiful bouquet of flowers. A note was tucked inside.

Dear AJ,

I can't write poems, so I'll have to let these flowers tell you thanks. You told me they have a language of their own. By the way, here is a check for your dog's tuition for obedience school. If you would like, I'd enjoy accompanying you when you take her for her first lesson.

Your Friend,

H. G. Gruen

AJ picked up the flowers. "Hm-m-m," she sighed smelling the fragrance. "Flowers certainly do have a beautiful language. I must tell Grandma we'll have to stop and pick up Brother Gruen in her "BMW" when we take Miranda to obedience school. I think she'll like that."